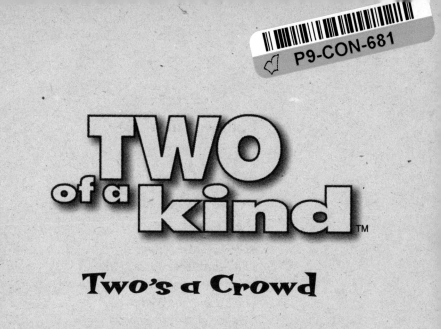

TWO of a kind™

Two's a Crowd

Look for more

titles:

TWO of a kind ™

Two's a Crowd

adapted by Judy Katschke
from the teleplays written by
Chip Keyes, David Hoge & Dan Cross
from the series created by
Robert Griffard & Howard Adler

HarperEntertainment
A PARACHUTE PRESS BOOK

A PARACHUTE PRESS BOOK

Parachute Publishing, L.L.C.
156 Fifth Avenue
Suite 325
New York, NY 10010

Published by

HarperEntertainment

A Division of HarperCollinsPublishers
10 East 53rd Street, New York, NY 10022-5299

For information address HarperCollins Publishers,
10 East 53rd Street, New York, NY 10022-5299.

ISBN 0-06-106577-3

First printing: October 1999

Printed in the United States of America

Visit HarperEntertainment on the World Wide Web at
www.harpercollins.com

10 9 8 7 6 5 4 3

CHAPTER ONE

"What do you mean, you don't want to go tonight?" twelve-year-old Ashley Burke demanded. She and her twin sister Mary-Kate were sitting by themselves in the school lunchroom.

Mary-Kate rolled up the sleeves of her bulky black sweater and unwrapped her tuna salad sandwich.

"Ashley, you know how I feel about the ballet," she said. "It's about as exciting as watching the spin cycle on the washing machine."

Ashley rolled her eyes. She and her twin had a lot in common, with one major exception: Mary-Kate was mad for sports, and Ashley was crazy about ballet!

"What would Carrie say if you didn't go?" Ashley asked. She placed a napkin neatly over her lap. "You know she got the tickets for both of us."

Just then, their friends Max and Brian plunked down their trays next to Mary-Kate and Ashley.

"Did you say *tickets*?" Max asked.

"As in . . . tickets to the opening Cubs game?" Brian asked excitedly. "Man. Your baby-sitter is even cooler than I thought."

"The Cubs game? *I wish*." Mary-Kate sighed. "Carrie got us tickets for some lame dance company."

Ashley frowned. No one insulted the Todd Tyler Dance Company. Not even her own twin!

"The Todd Tyler Dance Company is the greatest dance company in the entire world!" Ashley declared. "I saw them on TV last month and they were rolling around on the floor wrapped in gauze."

"I did that once," Brian said. He took a slurp of his grape soda. "When I sprained my ankle during softball practice."

Mary-Kate giggled.

Ashley shook her head. Totally hopeless. They just didn't get it. "That dance represents the pain and suffering of the modern world!" she said, jabbing the table with her finger.

"It represents a major yawn!" Mary-Kate countered.

Max tore open a small bag of chips. "Why did Carrie get you tickets to the ballet, anyway?" he asked. "I thought she liked baseball, basketball— you know, *fun* stuff!"

"Carrie likes the ballet, too," Mary-Kate said. She gave Ashley a wink. "But I won't hold it against her."

"Cute," Ashley said. She turned to Max and Brian. "Actually, Carrie bought the tickets to inspire me. My ballet recital is next Saturday. We're performing scenes from *Swan Lake*."

"*Your* ballet recital?" Mary-Kate groaned. "I suppose I have to sit through that, too."

Ashley smiled as she took a bite of her sandwich. She knew Mary-Kate was just pretending to complain. Not only did she come to all of Ashley's dance recitals, but she always showed up backstage with a bouquet of yellow roses—Ashley's favorite.

"Remember our deal, Mary-Kate," Ashley pointed out. "You come to my recital Saturday night, and I'll come to your basketball game on Sunday."

"A deal's a deal." Mary-Kate sighed. "But what does it have to do with the Todd Tyler Dance Company?"

"The Todd Tyler Dance Company?" Ashley heard a girl's voice squeal. "Did you say the Todd Tyler Dance Company?"

Ashley looked up. She saw Nicole Nemeth from her history class standing over the table. Nicole was wearing a charcoal gray sweater and black jeans. Her layered blond hair was clipped back by barrettes.

"Have you ever seen them?" Ashley asked Nicole.

Nicole placed her tray on the table. She sat down on an empty seat across from the twins.

"Are you kidding?" she cried. "My dad took me to see the Todd Tyler dancers when I was just seven years old. Ever since then, I've been totally hooked. I have Todd Tyler Dance Company posters plastered all over my room."

"Wow," Ashley said. "You're a real fan!" She knew Nicole had cool taste in clothes. Now it turned out she had cool taste in dance companies, too!

"Major!" Nicole declared. "I'd give anything to go to the ballet tonight, but my little brother doesn't want to go. It's not fair. He always gets his way."

"I know how you feel," Mary-Kate joked.

"Gee, Nicole," Ashley said. "That's too bad."

"I know," Nicole groaned. "I've been dreaming about that show so much, I do pliés in my sleep."

Ashley stared at Nicole. She couldn't believe there was someone who liked ballet as much as she did. She and Nicole had a lot in common!

"Hey, Nicole?" Mary-Kate said. "If you like Todd Tyler that much, do you want to go with Ashley to the show tonight?"

Nicole's mouth dropped open. Her blond hair bounced as she nodded her head. "You bet I do!"

Wait a minute, Ashley thought. *How can Mary-Kate make an offer like that? Carrie doesn't have an extra ticket!*

"Um, Mary-Kate?" Ashley said in a low voice. "Do the math. Carrie got us three tickets. One for her, one for you, and one for me."

"I know," Mary-Kate said. "Nicole can have *my* ticket."

"But what about Carrie?" Ashley asked her sister. "Wouldn't she be hurt if you gave your ticket to a stranger?"

"Nicole's not a stranger," Mary-Kate said. "She's in our history class."

"And Carrie knows I don't like ballet," Mary-Kate said. "She just gave me a ticket because we're twins. Like when Grandma Burke gives us matching sweaters for our birthday. It's just another twin thing."

Nicole leaned over the table and grinned.

"A twin thing!" she said. "That is so cool. You know, all my life I've wanted a twin sister. Someone I could do everything with."

"Not *everything*," Ashley said, grinning at Mary-Kate.

Mary-Kate took a slurp of her juice. "So what will it be, Nicole?" she asked. "Do you want my ticket or not?"

"I sure do!" Nicole declared. "But are you absolutely, positively sure, Mary-Kate?"

"You'll be doing me a favor," Mary-Kate said. "Who wants to see a bunch of people rolling around in gauze, anyway?"

Nicole gasped. "That dance represents the pain and suffering of the modern world!"

"Right on!" Ashley said. She turned to her sister. "Thanks, Mary-Kate."

Reaching across the table to give Nicole a high five, Ashley felt a shiver of excitement. She had just made a new friend. And as Carrie always said, you can never have too many friends—or pairs of shoes!

"The show starts at seven thirty," Ashley told Nicole. "Do you think you can meet Carrie and me at the Bay Theater at ten after seven?"

Nicole nodded excitedly. "I'll ask my mom to drop me off."

"I have a great idea," Ashley said. "Maybe after the show we can stop off for ice cream at the Super Scooper!"

"The Super Scooper?" Mary-Kate cried. "Ashley, that's my favorite place. You never go to the Super Scooper without me."

"I'll bring you home a pint of Bodacious Butterscotch," Ashley promised Mary-Kate quickly. But she didn't want to talk about ice cream right now. She wanted to talk about ballet!

"Nicole?" Ashley asked. "Do you think Peter Hernandez and Liz Woo will perform a pas de deux?"

"Oooh, I hope so," Nicole said. "The last time I saw Liz, she leaped almost ten feet in the air!"

"Ten feet?" Mary-Kate chuckled. "She should be playing basketball."

Ashley and Nicole stared at Mary-Kate.

"Basketball?" Ashley said.

"Why?" Nicole asked.

Mary-Kate rolled her eyes. "It's a joke!" She nudged Max, who was playing a handheld video game with Brian.

"A joke?" Max said, looking up. "Oh yeah. Ha-ha." He went back to his game.

"Oh," Ashley said. Couldn't Mary-Kate tell she and Nicole didn't want to talk about sports right now?

Ashley turned back to Nicole. "Guess what? I heard that Madame Celia LeMarcel is going to the show tonight."

"You mean the famous ballet star?" Nicole cried. "I knew it. Anybody who's *anybody* is going to be at that show tonight. I can't wait!"

Mary-Kate tugged at Ashley's sleeve.

"What?" Ashley asked, turning around.

"There's a special about killer sharks on TV tonight," Mary-Kate said. "Do you want me to tape it for you?"

"Killer sharks?" Ashley said, wrinkling her nose. Why did Mary-Kate keep interrupting? "I don't think so."

She turned to Nicole. "That reminds me—the company is also performing the dance of the Humpback Whales!"

"The Humpback Whales?" Nicole said. "Cool!"

Mary-Kate sighed. She picked up her juice and sandwich and stood up. "Come on, guys," she said to Max and Brian. "I think we're out of our league

8

here. Let's go find a corner and talk sports."

"See you around," Max said to Ashley and Nicole. "Let us know about that pain and suffering part. Sounds cool."

"Way cool," Brian said. He pushed his chair back and followed Max and Mary-Kate.

"Bye," Nicole called after them. "And thanks again, Mary-Kate!"

"Bye," Ashley echoed. She watched her sister walk away.

I hope Mary-Kate isn't having second thoughts about giving her ticket to Nicole, she thought.

Nah, she couldn't be, Ashley decided. *Mary-Kate would rather watch killer sharks than go to a dance show any day!*

So there's no reason for her to be upset. No reason at all!

CHAPTER TWO

"What happened to your pictures of the Backstreet Boys?" Mary-Kate asked Ashley in school the next morning. "And Carrot Cake, the horse of your dreams?"

The twins stood in front of their lockers. Ashley was taping pictures of ballet dancers on the inside of her locker door.

"Oh, I recycled those," Ashley said. She put an extra piece of tape on a picture of a prima ballerina. "Besides, Nicole told me she has pictures of dancers inside her locker, too."

"Gee. What a coincidence," Mary-Kate said. She had a feeling Nicole had something to do with this. After all, Ashley hadn't stopped talking about

Nicole since she and Carrie came home from the Todd Tyler Dance show last night. Mary-Kate had barely gotten a word in edgewise. She hadn't even been able to ask Ashley where her pint of Bodacious Butterscotch was!

"Did I tell you that Madame LeMarcel signed our programs after the show?" Ashley asked. She held up her black-and-white program. "Mine still smells like her perfume. I wonder what scent she wears."

"Eau de Toe Shoes?" Mary-Kate asked.

"Mary-Kate!" Ashley complained. "Don't ever let Nicole hear you say that. Madame LeMarcel is her hero!"

Nicole, Nicole, Nicole!

Mary-Kate couldn't believe it. Ashley had made other friends before. But she'd never gotten so tight with someone so fast.

"Tell me something I *want* to know," Mary-Kate said. She kneeled down and opened her locker. "Like what kind of ice cream sundaes did you wolf down at Super Scooper? Hot fudge? Marshmallow? Butterscotch—"

"The Super Scooper?" Ashley exclaimed. She waved her hand. "That place is for little kids."

"But you *love* that place," Mary-Kate protested. "Why didn't you go?"

"Because every three minutes the waiters put on stupid hats and sing 'Happy Birthday' at the top of their lungs," Ashley said. "It's totally embarrassing and annoying. Nicole thinks so, too."

Nicole again! Mary-Kate tried to keep her temper. "Where did you go instead?" she asked.

"Nicole told us about this cool new place called the Big Cheese!" Ashley said, her eyes shining. "They serve *twenty-five* different flavors of cheesecake."

"Cheesecake?" Mary-Kate exclaimed. She stood up and faced Ashley. "We took a vow never to eat cheesecake. It looks too squishy, remember?"

"Well, I tried it," Ashley said.

"How was it?" Mary-Kate asked.

"It's an acquired taste," Ashley explained. "Carrie had Cappuccino Swirl, I had Strawberry Sensation, and Nicole had Luscious Lemon Chiffon. Where else can you get wicked flavors like that?"

"At the Super Scooper!" Mary-Kate exclaimed. She took her math book out of her backpack and placed it in her locker. "And they give you a free hat."

"We're too old for goofy hats," Ashley said. "That's another reason we went to the Big Cheese."

"Fine," Mary-Kate said. "But I prefer my cheese grilled. With tomatoes and bacon."

"Hi, Ashley!"

Mary-Kate whipped around. Nicole was standing behind her with a big smile on her face.

"Oh, hey, Nicole," Ashley said, grinning. "I was just talking about you."

"And talking, and talking, and talking!" Mary-Kate muttered under her breath.

"Hi, Mary-Kate," Nicole said quickly. But she was still smiling at Ashley.

"So are we still going to Magna Records tonight, Nicole?" Ashley asked.

Nicole nodded. "My dad said he can drive us there."

"Super!" Ashley said.

Magna Records? Mary-Kate thought. *Since when?*

"I thought we were going to the movies this afternoon, Ashley," Mary-Kate said. "You know, to see that flick about the guy who finds an Egyptian mummy in his gym locker on prom night?"

"Oh, right. I forgot," Ashley said. "Well, Nicole wants to listen to some new CDs. You want to come with us?"

"Yeah," Nicole said, shrugging. "Want to come?"

Mary-Kate glanced at Ashley and Nicole. They didn't look like they wanted her to come. Not really.

"That's okay," Mary-Kate said. "The last time I went to Magna Records I found earwax in the headphones."

"Eww!" Nicole and Ashley cried at the same time.

"Come on, Nicole," Ashley said, grabbing Nicole's arm. "If we don't move it, we're going to be late for Spanish."

"Okay, Ashley," Nicole said. She gave Mary-Kate a little wave. "Adios, Mary-Kate!"

"Adios," Mary-Kate grumbled.

This is just too weird, she thought. *Yesterday Ashley wanted to go to the ballet with Nicole. That's all. Now she wants to go everywhere with her!*

Big deal, Mary-Kate told herself. *If Ashley can have her own friends, so can I.*

She turned around and saw Max and Brian standing by their lockers.

"Hey, guys!" Mary-Kate said, walking over. "What's up?"

"Oh, hi," Brian said. He blushed as he leaned over the picture of Alicia Silverstone taped inside his locker.

"Want to do something tonight?" Mary-Kate asked. "I thought we could go to the Super Scooper and pig out. It's Tuesday. Yo-yo night."

Max shook his head. "No can do. That new kid Doug invited us to his birthday party."

"A party?" Mary-Kate asked. Her eyes brightened. "Do you think I can come, too? I'll bring my Twister

14

game and some of Carrie's wicked guacamole."

Max and Brian looked at each other. They shook their heads.

"Sorry, Mary-Kate," Max said carefully. "But tonight it's just us guys."

"Yeah!" Brian said. He rubbed his hands together. "Three hours of male bonding and laser tag."

"You mean three hours of watching you duck!" Max joked. He looked over his shoulder and gulped. "Uh-oh. Eighth graders are coming!"

"Oh, no!" Brian said. He jammed his books inside his locker. "I don't want to get stuffed in a trash can again. Let's run for it!"

"Sorry, Mary-Kate," Max said, waving. "Don't let us stop you from going to the Super Scooper."

"Yeah," Brian called back. "Or maybe they deliver."

Mary-Kate leaned against a locker and sighed.

She had a weird feeling that Ashley and Nicole would be spending lots of afternoons together. And that meant lots of *lonely* afternoons for Mary-Kate!

Why did I have to give Nicole my ticket to the Todd Tyler Dance Company? Mary-Kate thought. *What in the world was I thinking?*

CHAPTER THREE

"Carrie! Mary-Kate!" Ashley called. She stopped in the entrance hall and hung up her jacket. "I'm back."

"Ashley!" Mary-Kate called from the living room. "Get in here quick. You've got to see this!"

"See what?" Ashley asked. She tossed her backpack on the hall table and hurried into the living room.

"Surprise!" Mary-Kate said. She was sitting on the sofa with cotton stuffed between her toes. Carrie was painting her toenails hot pink.

"A pedicure?" Ashley asked. "You?"

Mary-Kate nodded. Then she giggled. "That tickles, Carrie!"

"Hi, Ashley," Carrie said. She waved with the nail polish brush. "Want to join us for some serious styling?"

Mary-Kate waved her right foot. "I bought this new polish on the way home from school today. Guess what the name of the color is?"

"Pepto-Bismol?" Ashley joked.

"Very funny," Mary-Kate said with a grin. "It's called Pas de Deux Pink. That's a ballet word, isn't it?"

A ballet word? Ashley thought. *Since when does Mary-Kate care about ballet?*

"You can borrow some if you want to," Mary-Kate added.

"No, thanks," Ashley said. "Nicole says that pink nail polish is totally out. Especially on toes."

Mary-Kate frowned. "Well, *excuse* me!" she said. "What does Princess Nicole put on *her* toes—cheesecake?"

Carrie chuckled, but Ashley wasn't amused. How dare Mary-Kate insult her new friend!

"Nicole happens to be very cool," Ashley said. "When it comes to fashion, she's exactly like me."

"A mall rat?" Mary-Kate asked.

Carrie held up the nail polish bottle. "Well, I kind of like this shade. And as they say in the fashion

17

mags, when it comes to toes—anything goes."

"Thanks, Carrie," Mary-Kate smiled. She turned to Ashley. "Forget the polish. How was Magna Records? Did you buy a new CD?"

Ashley shook her head. "Magna Records was lame. We ended up going to see *Locker Shocker*."

Mary-Kate straightened up. "You mean the movie about the mummy in the gym locker? On prom night?"

"Yeah!" Ashley said. Her eyes lit up. "It was scary at first. But you should have seen what he looked like under all those bandages. He was *such* a hunk!"

Mary-Kate stood up. She hobbled over to Ashley with cotton-stuffed toes.

"Excuse me," Mary-Kate said angrily. "But we were supposed to see that movie *together*!"

"What's the big deal?" Ashley asked. "Nicole and I got bored at the record store. And you were right. There *was* earwax in one of the headphones."

Mary-Kate left a trail of cotton as she paced the living room floor. "You ditched me," she declared. "I can't believe it. You guys ditched me!"

Ashley stared at Mary-Kate. She didn't realize her sister would be that upset. And what for? All Ashley did was go to the movies with a friend.

Millions of kids did that every single day.

"You were the one who didn't want to go to Magna Records," Ashley said. "You said so yourself."

"But I wanted to see that movie and you went without me!" Mary-Kate declared. "That's ditching. And if you don't believe me, look it up in the dictionary!"

Mary-Kate wasn't the only one who was mad now. Ashley was annoyed, too.

"What's up with you, anyway, Mary-Kate?" Ashley demanded.

"What's up with me? What's up with you?" Mary-Kate cried. "Ever since that dumb dance show, all you want to talk about is Nicole. And she is such a dweeb!"

Carrie placed the nail polish bottle on the coffee table. She stood up and walked over to the twins.

"Mary-Kate, Ashley," Carrie said. "Can we scrap the low blows and just calm down? I'm sure there's some kind of solution to all this."

"There is," Mary-Kate said. She turned to Ashley. "Why don't you just do everything with your cool new friend Nicole from now on?"

Ashley blinked. *Why is Mary-Kate acting like such a jerk?* she thought. *And why should I even care?*

"Maybe I will!" Ashley said.

"Fine!" Mary-Kate said.

"Fine!" Ashley shot back.

Mary-Kate whirled around. She began stomping out of the living room.

"Wait, Mary-Kate!" Carrie called. "Don't go!"

"Why?" Mary-Kate asked over her shoulder.

Carrie pointed to Mary-Kate's feet. "Your toenails aren't dry yet."

"Who cares?" Mary-Kate grumbled. "Who wants to wear a color you can't even pronounce?"

After Mary-Kate left the living room, Ashley sat down on the sofa next to Carrie.

"I don't get it, Carrie," Ashley said. "Mary-Kate has been acting so weird ever since I went with Nicole to the dance show. Why is she being such a pain?"

Carrie leaned back and shrugged. "Maybe she feels a little left out," she said. "After all, the two of you have been best friends since you were born. It's all part of being a twin."

Ashley folded her arms and sighed.

"Carrie, if being a twin means having no friends of your own," she said, "then I'd rather *not* be a twin!"

CHAPTER FOUR

"Girls!" Kevin Burke called from the kitchen. "You're going to be late for school if you don't move it."

"Coming!" Mary-Kate called as she walked down the stairs. She entered the kitchen swinging her backpack. Ashley followed, carrying her books in front of her.

"Morning, Dad," Ashley said.

"Hey, Dad," Mary-Kate said.

Mary-Kate sat down next to Ashley. But she didn't say a word. She and her sister had hardly spoken the entire weekend.

That's because Ashley spent the whole weekend on the phone with Nicole, Mary-Kate thought.

"Good morning," Kevin said cheerily. He held

up a colorful cereal box. On it was a cartoon draw-
ing of a squirrel. "I bought this from that natural
food store Carrie always raves about. It's called
Squirrel Nuts."

"Squirrel Nuts?" Mary-Kate repeated.

"It's crunchy and very healthy," Kevin said. The
cereal made a rattling sound as he poured some into
the twins' bowls. "And guaranteed to keep you
bright-eyed and bushy-tailed!" Kevin winked.
"Get it? Bright-eyed and bushy . . . tailed . . . like a
squirrel."

Mary-Kate glanced at Ashley out of the corner of
her eye. She wasn't laughing either.

"Why don't you just eat your breakfast, girls?"
Kevin sighed.

"Dad?" Mary-Kate asked. "Can you please ask
Ashley to pass the milk?"

"And can you please tell Mary-Kate not to splash
me when she pours?" Ashley asked Kevin.

Kevin took a deep breath. "Ashley, pass the milk.
Mary-Kate, be careful not to splash Ashley."

"Okay, Dad," Mary-Kate said. "Now can you tell
Ashley to return the sweater she borrowed from
me? That is, if it's not stained with cheesecake?"

Ashley's face was red as she turned to Kevin.
"Tell Mary-Kate that I do not have her sweater," she

22

said. "I only wear the *latest* styles."

Mary-Kate felt her blood boil. "Dad? Could you please tell Ashley that she's being a total turkey?"

"Dad?" Ashley snapped. "Tell Mary-Kate—'I know you are, but what am I?'"

Kevin formed a T with his hands. "That's it! Time-out!" he cried. "What do you think I am? Western Union?"

Mary-Kate stared at their dad. It wasn't often that he raised his voice. But right now he looked very annoyed.

"Listen, girls," Kevin said, taking a deep breath. He sat down at the table and folded his hands. "I know you two are angry at each other, but we can't go on this way. You'll have to find a way to settle this disagreement without bickering."

The twins looked at one another.

"If you're hoping we'll patch up this fight, Dad," Ashley said, "don't bet on it."

"Yeah," Mary-Kate said. "It would be easier to patch up the *Titanic*."

Kevin stood up and paced the kitchen.

"What's become of this family?" he cried. Then he stopped and snapped his fingers. "Family— that's it!"

"What's it?" Mary-Kate asked.

"That's what our problem is," Kevin said. "We don't spend enough time as a family."

Ashley rolled her eyes. "But we're eating breakfast together right now," she said.

"That's not enough," Kevin said. "As soon as the day starts, we're off in different directions. I have my job. Mary-Kate, you have sports. And Ashley, you have dance lessons."

"And *Nicole*," Mary-Kate muttered.

"I heard that!" Ashley snapped.

Kevin raised his hands for attention. "Starting here, starting now, we are going to spend more time as a family."

"You mean like the Brady Bunch?" Mary-Kate groaned. The thought of Ashley and her holding a goofy frog-racing contest or something made her sick!

"Dad, you can't be serious!" Ashley cried.

"I've never been more serious in my life," Kevin said. "Let's start with something simple. I get out of work early today. Why don't you both come home straight from school, and we'll spend the whole afternoon together."

"Can't, Dad," Ashley said. "Nicole and I are supposed to go to the mall after school."

Goody for them, Mary-Kate thought angrily. *I*

happen to have plans, too!

"I'm going to practice shooting hoops with Max," Mary-Kate volunteered, thrusting her chin in the air. "My big basketball game is this weekend."

"Aha!" Kevin said. "This is exactly what I meant. Everyone scattering off in different directions."

Mary-Kate put down her spoon. "But, Dad—"

"No buts," Kevin said, holding up his hand. "Tonight the three of us are going to rent a movie, make some popcorn, and spend some time together as a family. And we're going to enjoy every minute of it!"

"Can Nicole come?" Ashley asked.

"*Nicole* isn't a member of the family," Mary-Kate snapped. Couldn't Ashley forget about Nicole for a moment?

"Okay," Ashley said with a sigh. "But I don't want salt or butter on my popcorn. Nicole said it's loaded with sodium and fat grams."

"Great!" Mary-Kate muttered. "Why don't we just chew on Styrofoam instead?"

"I will buy the popcorn, girls," Kevin said sternly. "And I'll also pick up the video on the way home from work."

The twins stood up. They placed their cereal bowls and juice glasses in the sink.

"Dad? Can you check to see if *Chop-Chop Cops* is in the video store?" Mary-Kate said. "That's the flick about those awesome martial arts detectives."

"Give me a break," Ashley complained. "The last thing I want to watch are a bunch of hairy, sweaty men jumping out of burning cars."

"Look, Ashley," Mary-Kate said. "I like action-adventure movies. Deal with it."

"And I like movies that broaden my outlook and enrich my mind," Ashley said.

"Like what?" Mary-Kate demanded.

"Anything with Matt Damon or Brad Pitt," Ashley said.

"Good-bye, girls!" Kevin said. "Have a good day at school. And don't forget to think 'togetherness'!"

As the twins headed out the door, Mary-Kate rolled her eyes. *I am not looking forward to another evening of listening to Ashley talk about Nicole*, she thought. This wasn't going to be togetherness. It was going to be torture.

CHAPTER
FIVE

Maybe Nicole's family will move, Mary-Kate thought. *Or better yet—maybe she'll get abducted by aliens. That ought to keep her busy for about a million light-years—*

"Earth to Mary-Kate!" Mary-Kate's math tutor, Taylor Donovan, called.

"Huh?" Mary-Kate gasped. She looked up from her math book. "Oh, sorry, Taylor. I was just thinking of subtracting."

Subtracting Nicole from Ashley's life!

"Well, my tutoring is finally paying off, Mary-Kate," Taylor said, looking at Mary-Kate's latest math test. "You really nailed those equations. You must be totally psyched."

"Oh, sure," Mary-Kate said. "It might not show on the outside. But inside—cartwheels."

"Hi, Taylor," Ashley said as she came into the living room. Her hair was swept up in a neat bun, and she was carrying her ballet bag. "I like your new haircut."

"You said that last week," Taylor said.

"Well, it's really holding up," Ashley said.

Mary-Kate rolled her eyes. Ashley had a major crush on Taylor. It was so annoying!

Ashley smiled at Mary-Kate. "So, Mary-Kate, how's the math? What are you up to now? Plus and minus signs?"

Now you've gone too far, Mary-Kate thought.

She gritted her teeth. If Ashley wanted to play rough, she could, too!

"Here's a math problem for you, Ashley," she said. "If a dozen girls like Taylor, and one more named Ashley likes him too, then—"

"Dad!" Ashley shouted at the top of her lungs. "I'm going to be late for ballet class!"

Mary-Kate giggled. Ashley didn't want Taylor to know about her crush.

"Ready or not, here I come!" Kevin said, hurrying into the living room. He fumbled through his pocket for his car keys. "Mary-Kate, Carrie is in the kitchen if you need anything. And after I drop Ashley off at ballet, I'm going to the college to do some paperwork."

"So much for togetherness, huh, Dad?" Mary-Kate asked.

"Don't remind me," Kevin groaned.

Mary-Kate didn't have to. Last night's family affair was a total mess. Kevin wanted to make everyone happy, so he brought home buttered popcorn for Mary-Kate and a romantic comedy for Ashley. After a few minutes, the twins were fighting about who got to sit in the recliner.

"Nice try though, Dad," Ashley said. She stood on her toes and did a pirouette. "Bye, Mary-Kate. Bye, Taylor."

She's making me dizzy, Mary-Kate thought, as her sister twirled out of the living room.

"I still can't get over how well you did on your test, Mary-Kate," Taylor said. "If I didn't know you better, I'd think you and Ashley pulled a switch on me again."

"Are you kidding?" Mary-Kate grumbled. "If I twirled around the room like that, I'd lose my lunch."

"Thanks for sharing," Taylor said. He stood up and began packing his things. "But you girls could really fool some people if you wanted to."

Mary-Kate perked up.

Fool some people? she thought. *Hey, if I could fool a smart guy like Taylor, maybe I can fool a dweeb like Nicole!*

"See you, Mary-Kate," Taylor said. He gave a thumbs-up sign. "And keep up the great work."

Mary-Kate waited for Taylor to leave. When she heard the door slam, she raced to the phone.

"If *I* can't lose Nicole," she said under her breath, "maybe *Ashley* can."

Mary-Kate found Nicole's name on the speed-dial list. She pressed it and waited as the phone rang twice.

"Hello?" Nicole answered.

Mary-Kate cleared her throat. She forced herself to sound perky.

"Hi, Nicole!" Mary-Kate said. "It's me, Ashley. Can you come over? I've got something we need to talk about."

"Is it about the party that's coming up?" Nicole asked.

Mary-Kate made a face. What party? "Sort of," she answered slowly. "Can you come over now?"

"You bet!" Nicole said. "I'll be over in twenty minutes."

"Super!" Mary-Kate said. "See you soon."

She smiled as she hung up the phone. Of all her plans, this was the craziest. So crazy that it had to work!

"Carrie?" she said, popping her head into the kitchen. "When the doorbell rings, would you let me get it? I'm expecting a friend."

"A friend?" Carrie looked up from her college textbook and smiled. "Mary-Kate, that's great. See? You can have your own friends, too. Just like Ashley!"

"*Exactly* like Ashley!" Mary-Kate said.

She ran upstairs and quickly changed into Ashley's beige V-necked sweater and black capri pants. Then she combed her hair in a center part and fastened it with two pink-and-silver butterfly barrettes.

"Perfect," Mary-Kate whispered into the mirror.

Ding-dong!

Mary-Kate's heart skipped a beat. Nicole had arrived sooner than she expected. She slipped her feet into Ashley's sandals and stampeded down the stairs.

"Hi, Nicole," Mary-Kate sang in her most Ashley-like voice.

"Hey, Ashley," Nicole said. She held out a book.

"Look! I brought over my book about the Todd Tyler Dance Company!"

Mary-Kate took the big, glossy book. She forced herself to smile. "Todd Tyler?" she said. "Way cool."

"I still can't stop thinking about the show the other night," Nicole said. "What was your favorite part, Ashley?"

My favorite part? Mary-Kate thought. *Uh-oh.*

"Um," Mary-Kate said. "When the main guy . . . jumped in the air and wiggled his feet?"

"The entrechat!" Nicole exclaimed. "That was my favorite part, too!"

"No way!" Mary-Kate squealed, trying to cover her nervousness. She began to have second thoughts. What if she couldn't keep up the act? It wasn't easy being someone else—even if that someone else was your own twin.

And what about Nicole? Mary-Kate wondered. *What if this trick really freaks her out? What if she shuts herself in her room? Or runs away and joins the circus? What if—*

"Ashley?" Nicole interrupted her thoughts. "You said you have something to talk about?"

"Yes!" Mary-Kate said quickly. "Why don't we go upstairs to my room?"

"Okay," Nicole said.

Nicole followed Mary-Kate as she walked up the stairs. When she opened the door to the twins' bedroom, Nicole gasped.

"What's the matter?" Mary-Kate asked.

"It's true!" Nicole said.

"What's true?" Mary-Kate asked, confused.

"Mary-Kate's side of the room *is* a pigsty!" Nicole giggled. "Oink, oink, oink!"

Mary-Kate felt her cheeks burn. Ashley and Nicole didn't just talk about ballet and clothes— they talked about *her!*

I can't believe Ashley would say something so mean about me behind my back, Mary-Kate thought. *Even if it is true! I'm going through with this exactly as planned!*

"I always wanted a twin sister," Nicole chattered on. "But not if she's messy like this."

Mary-Kate balled her hands into fists. "Nicole—"

"I'll bet her bed is lumpy, too," Nicole laughed. "And her clothes closet must be a disaster."

"Nicole!" Mary-Kate yelled.

Nicole stared at Mary-Kate. "What?"

Mary-Kate waved her hand in the direction of Ashley's bed. "Have a seat, please."

"Sure."

Nicole sat down on Ashley's bed. She picked up

one of Ashley's stuffed animals and bounced it on her lap.

"So," Nicole said. "What do you want to talk about? Do you really think Kyle Martin has a crush on you?"

Oh, brother. Mary-Kate tried hard not to groan. *Now it's Kyle?*

"This isn't easy, Nicole," Mary-Kate said. She took a deep breath. "But I've decided we can't be friends anymore."

Nicole's eyes flew wide open. She clutched the stuffed giraffe. "What?" she whispered.

"It's not you, it's me!" Mary-Kate said. "I'm selfish and cold. I even hate little animals."

Nicole stared at the dozens of stuffed animals on Ashley's bed. "You could have fooled me!"

Mary-Kate grabbed an armful of stuffed animals. She dumped them on her own bed.

"Those are Mary-Kate's," she said quickly. "They're always migrating."

"I don't understand this," Nicole said, shaking her head. "We're great friends, Ashley. We have so much fun together. We both love clothes and ballet and—"

"But I'm a dead end," Mary-Kate said dramatically. "Stick with me and you're on a bus to nowhere."

"I don't care," Nicole said. She smiled warmly. "I like you, Ashley."

Mary-Kate started to panic. Nicole was tough to get through to.

"You're not getting this!" Mary-Kate said. "I don't want to be your friend anymore because . . . because . . ."

"Because what?" Nicole asked, jumping up from the bed.

"Because of your hair!" Mary-Kate blurted out.

Nicole touched her long, layered locks. "My hair?"

"I hate it!" Mary-Kate said.

Nicole's eyes filled with tears.

"But this style was in the last issue of *Teen World Magazine*," Nicole said. "Didn't you see it?"

"You mean in that article called 'Beating Bad Hair Days'?" Mary-Kate asked with a snort. She put her hands on her hips. "Look, Nicole. Your 'do' just doesn't cut it. In fact, maybe that's what you should do with your hair. Cut it."

Nicole's chin began to quiver. She wrapped her arms around her head and ran toward the door.

"I thought you were my best friend, Ashley!" Nicole sniffed over her shoulder.

Mary-Kate felt a stab of guilt. *Uh-oh, I've made her*

cry! she thought. But it was too late to back out now.

"I guess not," Mary-Kate said. "In fact, I think it would be best if we never spoke again."

Nicole choked back a sob and flew out the door. Mary-Kate could hear Nicole's feet pounding down the stairs.

"Um—nothing personal, of course!" Mary-Kate called after her. She closed the door and leaned against it.

"Yes!" she whispered under her breath. "Mission accomplished."

As she kicked off Ashley's sandals, Mary-Kate wondered if she had gone too far. She didn't want to hurt Nicole's feelings—just make her go away. But when she remembered the mean things Nicole said about her, she changed her mind.

The score is tied, Mary-Kate thought. *And Nicole Nemeth is out of the game!*

CHAPTER SIX

"Hi, Nicole!" Ashley said the next morning.

Nicole looked over her shoulder as she slipped her science project into her locker. "Ashley," she said curtly.

That's weird, Ashley thought. *Nicole is usually a lot friendlier than this.*

Ashley glanced at Mary-Kate. Her sister shrugged.

I'll try again, Ashley thought.

"How are you doing?" she asked.

"Oh, like you care," Nicole snapped.

"What are you talking about?" Ashley exclaimed.

Nicole reached into her locker. She pulled out a fashion magazine and held it up.

"See her hair?" Nicole demanded.

Ashley stared at the supermodel with the dark, shaggy hair. "Yeah, so?"

"Mine is exactly like hers," Nicole said. "And she's making millions of bucks and dating a rock star."

Nicole tossed the magazine back in her locker and slammed it shut. "This is the last time we will ever speak again, Ashley Burke. The last time."

"Nicole!" Ashley called as Nicole walked away. "Wait up!"

But Nicole didn't stop or turn around. She just kept walking down the hall.

"What's with her?" Ashley asked Mary-Kate.

"Who knows?" Mary-Kate said. "Maybe she found a twig in her Squirrel Nuts. I wouldn't worry about it if I were you."

But Ashley *was* worried. *How can I have a best friend one day,* she wondered, *and lose her the next?*

That day in her classes, Ashley couldn't concentrate on math, science, or Spanish. All she could think about was Nicole. Why was she so mad? Was it something Ashley did? Or said?

Ashley had no idea. But she was going to find out.

"I don't know what happened, Carrie," Ashley said after school. "I was standing by my locker, and the next thing I know, Nicole comes over and starts yelling about her hair."

Carrie looked up from the brownies she was cutting on the kitchen table. "Are you sure you didn't say anything to her?" she asked.

"No," Ashley said. "I hadn't seen her since gym class yesterday, and we got along great then."

Mary-Kate pinched a walnut off a brownie. "Maybe you hogged the volleyball. Or whacked her in the face during jumping jacks."

"I did nothing of the kind," Ashley insisted.

Carrie placed a brownie on each of the twins' plates. "I wouldn't take it personally, Ashley. It sounds like she was just having a bad hair day. That can bring out the worst in people, you know."

"Maybe," Ashley said. She felt so bad she couldn't even eat Carrie's nutty triple-fudge brownies.

"Hey!" Mary-Kate said. She licked her chocolaty fingers. "I know what would make you feel better, Ashley. How about a trip to the mall?"

"The mall?" Ashley said. She shook her head. "Now I'm really confused. You never want to go to the mall, Mary-Kate. Unless it's for a corn dog on a stick."

"A person can change," Mary-Kate said, shrugging. "Besides, I want to get a brand-new toenail polish. Hot pink is so totally out."

Why is Mary-Kate being so nice all of a sudden?
Ashley wondered. *Just yesterday she was practically
biting my head off.*

"Okay," Ashley said. "I'll go."

"Great," Mary-Kate said. She stood up and
headed for the door. "I'll run upstairs and wash my
hands. Then I'll get our jackets."

"Wow," Carrie said when Mary-Kate was out of
the kitchen. "Does this mean you two declared a
truce?"

"I guess so," Ashley said. "I wonder why Mary-
Kate is so cheery all of a sudden. I thought she was
still mad at me."

"Maybe her new friend has something to do with
it," Carrie said.

New friend? Ashley thought. *Mary-Kate?*

"Since when does Mary-Kate have a new
friend?" Ashley asked.

"Since yesterday afternoon," Carrie explained.
"She came over while you were still at ballet class."

"Who is she?" Ashley asked.

"I don't know," Carrie admitted. "Mary-Kate got
the door and they ran straight up to your room."

The phone rang. Carrie wiped her hands on a
towel and reached for it.

"Burke residence," she said. "Uh, hold on."

Carrie put her hand over the receiver. "Ashley, it's Nicole," she whispered.

Nicole? All right!

Ashley jumped up and grabbed the phone. "Hi, Nicole!"

"Hello, Ashley," Nicole said.

Ashley frowned. Nicole's voice was still as cold as a frozen slushy.

"I'll get right to the point," Nicole said. "I want my Todd Tyler Dance Company book back."

Ashley wrinkled her nose. "Your Todd Tyler book? I don't have your Todd Tyler book."

"Don't play games with me, Ashley," Nicole snapped. "I gave you the book when I came over yesterday afternoon."

Yesterday afternoon? Ashley thought. *That's impossible.*

"But I wasn't even here yesterday afternoon!" she insisted. "I was at ballet class."

"No, you weren't," Nicole said. "You took my book, then you insulted my hair."

Ashley was convinced things couldn't get weirder. She knew she was at dance class yesterday—she even had a blister on her big toe to prove it. And the only people in the house were Carrie and Mary-Kate and her new friend—

New friend! Suddenly it clicked.

Maybe that new friend was Nicole, Ashley thought.
And maybe Mary-Kate was pretending to be me!

*Mary-Kate was jealous of Nicole—and she figured out
a way to get rid of her!*

"Creep!" Ashley muttered.

"What did you just call me?" Nicole demanded.

Ashley jumped. She stared at the phone.

"Oh, not you, Nicole," Ashley said quickly. "I
had someone else in mind . . . I'll call you back."

"Don't bother," Nicole muttered.

Ashley heard a click at the other end. She hung
up her own receiver with a bang.

So that's it, Ashley thought. *Mary-Kate insulted
Nicole and now Nicole thinks it was me!*

Ashley was so mad that she could practically feel
steam coming out of her ears.

"Mary-Kate played a sneaky trick on me," she
muttered under her breath. "And I'm going to make
sure she never plays one again!"

CHAPTER SEVEN

"Hi, Mary-Kate," Kevin said as he walked into the entry hallway. He put his briefcase on the floor.

"Hi, Dad!" Mary-Kate said, running down the stairs. She reached for her jacket on the coatrack. Then she grabbed Ashley's.

"Where are you off to?" Kevin asked, sifting through the mail on the hall table.

Mary-Kate couldn't wait to tell her dad the good news.

"Ashley and I are going to the mall," she said excitedly. "Just like old times. Isn't that neat?"

"It sure is!" Kevin said. "I'm glad you're doing stuff together again."

Mary-Kate nodded. "Things are going great, Dad.

In fact, the fight of the century is practically history."

Holding the jackets in both arms, Mary-Kate turned around. Then she gasped.

Standing behind her and looking meaner than a pitbull was Ashley!

"You're toast!" Ashley shouted.

Mary-Kate jumped to the side as Ashley lunged at her. Then she ran into the kitchen.

"You ruined my life!" Ashley screamed as she chased Mary-Kate around the breakfast table.

Oh, no! Mary-Kate thought as she ran. *Ashley must have found out about my trick. But how?*

"Does this mean we're not going to the mall?" Mary-Kate shouted over her shoulder.

"Arrrrgh!" Ashley growled, swinging her fists.

Kevin and Carrie ran into the kitchen.

"Hey, you guys!" Carrie cried.

"Stop it right now!" Kevin ordered.

Kevin grabbed Ashley, and Mary-Kate ran behind Carrie.

"You liar!" Ashley screamed. "I hate you!"

"Ashley, that's enough," Kevin said, holding her back. "What's gotten into you?"

"Mary-Kate pretended to be me and insulted Nicole," Ashley said. "Now Nicole thinks I did it and she won't even speak to me."

So that's who was on the phone when it rang—Nicole! Mary-Kate thought. *Why didn't I pick up the phone?*

"Mary-Kate?" Kevin asked.

Mary-Kate peeked out from behind Carrie.

"Why would you do something like that?" Kevin asked.

"Uh . . . temporary insanity?" Mary-Kate squeaked. She glanced at Ashley and gulped. Her sister had never looked so mad in her life.

"Listen, you guys," Carrie said. "If you two have a problem, then you need to talk about it."

"Oh, I'll talk about it!" Ashley said. "Right after I wipe the floor with Mary-Kate!"

"Help!" Mary-Kate yelled from behind Carrie. Her sister meant business!

"Stop it!" Kevin said. He turned to Mary-Kate. "Mary-Kate, I think you have some explaining to do. Why did you do it?"

Uh-oh, Mary-Kate thought. *Trouble city!*

"I don't know," she said softly.

"She did it because she hates Nicole," Ashley said.

"I do not," Mary-Kate declared.

"Yes, you do," Ashley said. "You hate her because she's cooler than you and more fun to be around."

The words hit Mary-Kate like a ton of bricks. *So*

45

that's how Ashley really feels about me! She felt her eyes fill with tears. "Oh, really?" she said. "Then why don't you just do everything with Nicole from now on?"

"Maybe I will!" Ashley shouted.

"Good!" Mary-Kate yelled. "Because if we weren't twins, we wouldn't be friends, anyway. We have nothing in common!"

"If you feel that way," Ashley said angrily, "then let's *not* be twins anymore. I want a divorce!"

"Sounds good to me!" Mary-Kate said. "Then we won't have to have the same birthday parties. And best of all, I won't have to go to your stupid ballet!"

"And I won't have to go to your sweaty basketball game!" Ashley snapped back.

"Wait a minute, you guys!" Carrie said. "How can you not be twins anymore?"

"You'll always be twins," Kevin said. "Even I can't tell you apart sometimes."

"It's easy, Dad," Ashley said. She glared at Mary-Kate. "I'm the one with the *honest* face!"

"Girls," Kevin said. He shook his head. "This fight of yours has *got* to stop."

"Why, Dad?" Mary-Kate said. She narrowed her eyes at Ashley. "If you ask me, this twin divorce is the best idea Ashley's had in a long time!"

CHAPTER EIGHT

"Dad, can you give us a hand in here, please?" Ashley called from the bedroom.

"Sure, Ashley," Kevin called back from the hall. "I'll be right there."

But when Kevin appeared at the door he froze. He stepped into the room and looked around.

"Whoa!" Kevin gasped.

Ashley turned away from the closet she was dusting. She knew her father would come upstairs sooner or later.

"Something wrong, Dad?" she asked, twirling her feather duster. "You look like you just saw a ghost."

"You bet there's something wrong!" Kevin cried. He pointed to Mary-Kate, who was loading a cardboard box with trophies. "Mary-Kate is packing boxes. And you're dusting Mary-Kate's side of the closet. Can someone please tell me what's going on in here?"

"Mary-Kate is moving up to the attic," Ashley said.

"Excuse me," Mary-Kate said. She placed her hands on her hips. "I like to refer to it as the penthouse!"

Ashley rolled her eyes. Mary-Kate had always called the attic the rec room. Now it was the penthouse. La-dee-da!

"Whatever." Ashley waved her hand over the closet. "All I know is that I'm going to have closet space for a change. Oh, thank you, Universe!"

"But, girls," Kevin said. "You always shared a room. In fact, you *liked* sharing a room."

"Change is good, Dad," Ashley said. "That's what you're always telling us."

Kevin ran his hand through his hair and sighed. "Mary-Kate, Ashley," he said. "I know you two had a little fight. But can't you settle it some other way? Like draw a line down the middle of the room?"

"Oh, Dad!" Ashley said. "We already did that—a

long time ago, when we were kids."

Mary-Kate giggled.

"What's so funny?" Ashley asked.

"Remember when your bubble bath oozed over the borderline?" Mary-Kate asked.

"Oh, yeah!" Ashley said, smiling slowly. How could she forget the Great Bubble Bath Disaster?

"Bubble bath?" Kevin raised an eyebrow. "Here in your bedroom?"

"Don't you remember, Dad?" Ashley asked. "We were six years old. I was trying to take a bubble bath in a wading pool right here in our room. But I poured in a whole box of Mister Sudsy!"

Mary-Kate was still laughing as she walked over to Ashley. "There were so many bubbles—Mom had to suck them all out with a vacuum cleaner! Remember?"

"How could I forget?" Ashley laughed.

But then she stopped. Now wasn't the time for warm and fuzzy memories. Not when they were about to call it splitsville!

Mary-Kate stopped laughing, too. "Those bubbles were a total mess," she grumbled.

"At least they cleaned *your* side of the room," Ashley muttered.

She returned to the closet. Mary-Kate began

loading a box with paperback books.

"Um, girls," Kevin said quickly. He waved his hand around the room. "What about all of your things?"

"Our things?" Ashley asked.

"You know, the stuff you've·always shared," Kevin said. He walked around the room pointing out objects. "Your inflatable Godzilla, your electric-blue lava lamp . . . your Musical Magic Eight Ball . . . your—"

He looked into a shoebox with red hearts pasted on it. "Pictures of Ben Affleck?" he asked.

Blushing, Ashley grabbed the shoebox. "Don't worry, Dad. We've taken all those things into consideration."

"And it's all here in writing!" Mary-Kate said, holding up a piece of paper.

Kevin took the sheet of paper. He looked at it and blinked. "A custody agreement?"

"You and Carrie told us to work things out." Ashley shrugged. "So we did."

"I get the Walkman every *even* day," Mary-Kate explained.

"And I get the curling iron every *odd* day," Ashley said.

Mary-Kate snickered. "Every day you style your

hair is an odd day, Ashley."

Ashley glared at Mary-Kate. Wasn't it enough that her sister tried to break up a perfectly good friendship? Ashley was just lucky that Nicole had forgiven her after she found out what really happened.

Ashley was in no mood to put up with Mary-Kate's insults.

"That does it!" Ashley cried. She turned to her father and planted her hands on her hips. "I want Mary-Kate's bed out of here by tonight!"

"Tonight?" Kevin cried.

Mary-Kate pointed to the shoebox. "But we still haven't figured out how to split Ben!"

"Tonight!" Ashley repeated.

"Fine with me," Mary-Kate said. She picked up an armload of rolled-up posters and stomped out of the room.

"Mary-Kate," Kevin called, running after her. "Wait!"

When Ashley was alone, she looked around the room. Without Mary-Kate's sports posters and piles of clothes, the room seemed practically empty.

All this space—just for me! Ashley thought. *I won't miss that junk at all.*

And I certainly won't miss Mary-Kate!

CHAPTER NINE

"Are you serious?" Nicole asked Ashley the next afternoon. She looked around Ashley's room. "Did Mary-Kate really move out of here?"

Ashley nodded and threw a bag on the bed. She and Nicole were just back from a trip to the mall. "Last night. At eight forty-five."

"Wow," Nicole said. "What did your dad say?"

Ashley looked over her shoulder to see if Kevin was around. "I think he's really hurting bad," she whispered.

"Aw," Nicole said, looking sympathetic. "Because you two are mad at each other?"

"No," Ashley said. "Because he had to lug Mary-Kate's beanbag chair on his back!"

"Ouch," Nicole said. "So what's it like finally having your own room?"

"What's it like?" Ashley repeated. She thought about last night. Being alone felt so weird that she'd hardly slept a wink.

"It's cool!" Ashley lied. "I *love* having my own room!"

Ashley motioned to Nicole and began walking up the stairs to the attic. They reached the top and stopped in front of Mary-Kate's door.

"Why are we going up here?" Nicole asked.

"Because it's my day to get the curling iron, that's why," Ashley said. "It's part of our custody agreement."

Ashley was about to knock on Mary-Kate's door when she heard music coming from inside.

"Wow," Nicole said. She put her hands over her ears. "Mary-Kate sure likes her music loud."

That's funny, Ashley thought, pressing her ear against the door. *It sounds like there are kids inside, too. Lots of kids!*

"Mary-Kate," Ashley called.

No answer.

"Mary-Kate!" she called again, pounding on the door. "Open up!"

After a few seconds Mary-Kate opened the door

a crack. She peeked out into the hall.

"Oh, Ashley, Nicole," Mary-Kate said. "What can I do for you?"

"What's going on in there?" Ashley asked.

Mary-Kate smiled as she swung the door wide open. "See for yourself," she said.

Ashley gasped. The attic was filled with kids dancing and passing around bowls of nacho chips and pretzels. Crepe paper and balloons hung from the ceiling.

"I just invited a few friends over," Mary-Kate explained.

"You're having a party?" Ashley gasped. How could Mary-Kate have a party and not tell her about it?

Mary-Kate nodded as a balloon floated over her head. "It's kind of an 'attic-warming' party. I mean—*penthouse*-warming."

Jennifer Dilber, the twins' friend from school, squeezed past Ashley and Nicole. She was holding a plant with a pink ribbon tied around the pot.

"Hi, Jennifer," Ashley said.

"Oh, hi, Ashley," Jennifer said. She held the plant out to Mary-Kate. "I brought this for your new room, Mary-Kate."

Ashley was stunned. Jennifer Dilber was more

her friend than she was Mary-Kate's.

"Thanks, Jennifer," Mary-Kate said. "It'll look great next to my lava lamp."

"You mean *our* lava lamp!" Ashley corrected.

Brian leaned out the door. He was holding a fistful of potato chips covered in dip. "Great party, Mary-Kate. And this green dip is awesome. What is it?"

"Spinach," Mary-Kate said.

"Spinach?" Brian gagged. He yelled over his shoulder. "Green alert! Green alert! The dip is tainted with vegetables!"

Mary-Kate smiled and rolled her eyes.

"Boys!" she chuckled. Then she waved Jennifer into the attic. "Come on in, Jennifer. There's a buffet by the window."

I'm going in, too, Ashley thought. She pulled Nicole's hand and tried to follow Jennifer into the attic.

"And just where do you think you're going?" Mary-Kate asked, holding out her hand.

"To your party," Ashley said. She glanced over her shoulder. "Come on, Nicole."

"I'm sorry," Mary-Kate said. "But this is an invitation-only party."

Ashley couldn't believe her ears. Since when did *she* need an invitation?

"But I'm your twin," Ashley complained.

Mary-Kate cleared her throat. "If I remember correctly, we stopped being twins about"—she looked at her watch—"twenty-two hours ago."

"Not twins anymore?" Nicole gasped. She looked thrilled. "And I thought you just moved out."

"Besides, Ashley," Mary-Kate went on. "I figured you were busy with your new life. And your new friend Nicole."

So that's it, Ashley thought. *So that's what this little party is all about—revenge!*

Ashley stood on her toes and tried to look over Mary-Kate's shoulder into the attic. "Those are my friends, too, you know!"

"I guess we'll have to work something out," Mary-Kate sighed. "I know. You get Max and Brian on even days. Except when I need them for softball."

"Hey, Mary-Kate!" Max called from the room. "We want to do the limbo. Can we use your hockey stick?"

"Sure, Max!" Mary-Kate called back. She turned to Ashley. "I have to get back to my guests now."

"Wait!" Ashley said. "I came up here for a reason. It's my day to get the curling iron."

"Okay," Mary-Kate said. "Don't go away."

Mary-Kate ran into her room. When she came back, she handed Ashley the curling iron.

"Why are there crumbs in it?" Ashley asked.

"We were using it to heat hot dog buns," Mary-Kate said. "It really does the trick."

Ashley made a face. She handed the curling iron back to Mary-Kate. "That's okay. You can keep it."

"Yo, Mary-Kate!" a voice called from inside. "Who's at the door? The pizza-delivery guy?"

"No, just someone who used to be my twin," Mary-Kate called back. She smiled at Ashley and Nicole. "I really have to go now. See you!"

"But—"

SLAM!

Ashley took a few steps back. She stared at the closed door and shook her head.

"I can't believe it," Ashley said. "Mary-Kate and I never had separate parties before."

"Hey, don't worry, Ashley," Nicole said. She gave Ashley a pat on the back. "I'll be your twin from now on."

Ashley turned to Nicole. "You'll be my—what?"

"Your twin!" Nicole said excitedly.

Ashley blinked hard. Was Nicole serious?

"That's real cute, Nicole," Ashley said. She tilted

her head. "But you're joking. Aren't you?"

"Of course not!" Nicole said, her eyes shining. "I've never been so serious in my whole life. You know how much I've always wanted a sister. Now's my chance!"

"But, Nicole—"

"Besides," Nicole said. "You and Mary-Kate aren't twins anymore. You said so yourself."

Ashley listened to the music coming from Mary-Kate's party. The one she wasn't invited to.

That's right, Ashley thought. *We're not twins anymore.*

And as long as Mary-Kate plays this game, so will I!

CHAPTER TEN

"Ashley, open up!" Mary-Kate called. She knocked on Ashley's bedroom door. "It's me!"

After a few seconds, Ashley opened the door. The headphones of her Walkman were hanging around her neck.

"I couldn't hear you. I had my Screaming Mimis tape on," Ashley said. "What do you want?"

Mary-Kate grinned as she held out a big blue bowl. "I come bearing leftovers."

And to see how you're doing, Mary-Kate thought. Part of her was happy that Ashley wasn't at the party—and part of her wanted to tell Ashley all about it!

Ashley peered into the bowl. "What's in there?"

"It's my own brand of party mix," Mary-Kate explained. "I tossed in leftover cheese curls, chocolate fudge cookies, nacho chips, and sour watermelon worms."

"I'll pass." Ashley sighed. She leaned against the door frame. "How was your party, anyway? The one you banned me from?"

"Just great," Mary-Kate said. "Tommy Rizzo and Matt Gallagher got stuck together playing Twister. They won first prize."

"For Twister?" Ashley asked.

"No," Mary-Kate said. She smiled. "For best imitation of a pretzel."

Ashley pinched a cheese curl from the bowl and popped it in her mouth. "I suppose you'll have to clean up the mess from your party," she said. "Oh, I forgot. You *live* in the attic now. That means you'll be *leaving* it a mess."

Mary-Kate narrowed her eyes. There was no use being friendly to Ashley. She always made some dumb comment.

"Ha, ha. Very funny, Ashley," she said. "That penthouse is the best thing that's ever happened to me."

"Well, I don't believe it," Ashley said.

"Why not?" Mary-Kate asked.

"Because the attic is the creepiest place in the whole house," Ashley said.

"Creepy?" Mary-Kate cried. "That attic used to be our rec room. You were up there all the time."

"Oh, the attic is a nice place to visit," Ashley said. "But I wouldn't want to spend the whole night there. Especially a night like this. Did you hear the storm brewing outside?"

"Storm?" Mary-Kate gulped. Ever since she was little, thunderstorms had given her goosebumps. "There's going to be a storm? Tonight?"

Ashley nodded. "It's a great night for the ducks—oh, and bats, of course."

"*Bats*?" Mary-Kate squeaked.

"You mean you haven't heard them?" Ashley asked. "A few weeks ago when I was up in the attic I saw something flying against the ceiling. Then I heard this flap, flap, flapping noise up in the rafters. And then this weird squeaky sound. Sort of like eeeek, eeeek, eeeek!"

Mary-Kate clutched the bowl. She remembered looking at bats in her science book. They were brown and leathery with pointed fangs. Long, dripping, pointed fangs!

"So what if there's a little bat up there?" Mary-Kate forced herself to say. "He's probably more scared of me than I am of him."

"Oh, sure," Ashley said, leaning against the door frame. "Until the sun goes down, and he turns into a vampire."

"A vampire?" Mary-Kate cried.

"You heard me," Ashley said. "In fact, if you think Max and Brian can be pains in the neck—wait until you meet Count Dracula!"

"You're crazy!" Mary-Kate said. She felt the hairs on her arm stick up. "There are no bats in my room. And especially no vampires!"

"Of course, we wouldn't know if there were," Ashley said. "You're up there all alone. Nobody would hear you scream."

Just appear calm, Mary-Kate thought. *Even though the party mix is rattling in your hands.*

"Nice try, Ashley," Mary-Kate said. "But you can't scare me. Nothing scares me!"

Crash!

A clap of thunder made Mary-Kate jump almost ten feet. Watermelon worms and cheese curls flew out of the bowl.

Ashley giggled. "Nothing, huh?"

"Party food makes me jumpy," Mary-Kate said, still shaking. "I'm funny that way."

"I'm going to bed," Ashley said, closing the door.

"Just don't forget to cover your head tonight. Bats love a good head of hair."

"You can't scare me!" Mary-Kate yelled through the door. She looked up toward the attic and gulped. "Not . . . much."

The storm got worse as the night wore on.

Mary-Kate lay in bed with a flowered scarf wrapped around her head.

What was that? she wondered as a strange brushing sound filled the room. *What if Ashley is right? What if there are bats in the attic?*

A huge flash of lightning lit up her attic room. The stuffed clown on her bookcase grinned at her creepily.

My old room never seemed this scary, Mary-Kate thought. *But maybe that's because I was never alone. Ashley was always with me.*

Scrape!

There was that sound again!

Mary-Kate squirmed as a dark shadow loomed against the windowpane. It was too big to be a bat.

But not too big to be a vampire!

Mary-Kate reached under her covers and pulled out a sprinkle-can of powdered garlic.

Of course, I don't really believe in vampires, she

thought. *But just in case, I want to be prepared. If Ashley were here, she'd probably do the same thing!*

Mary-Kate slipped quietly out of bed.

Vampires in the movies hate this stuff, she thought as she unscrewed the lid. *I'll cover him with garlic like a meatball hero. That ought to bring him to his knees!*

Clutching the can of garlic, Mary-Kate ran to the window. She yanked back the shade and pulled up the window.

"Take that, you blood-sucking creep in a cape!" Powdered garlic shot out of the can like a torpedo. A breeze blew it back in her face.

Coughing, Mary-Kate stepped back. She peered through the stinky cloud of garlic and sighed.

It wasn't a vampire. Or a bat. Just a tree branch.

"I'm safe," Mary-Kate whispered. She wrinkled her nose. "But my room stinks."

Another clap of thunder sent her springing to her bed. She pulled the covers completely over her head.

Being alone on a night like this is the pits, she thought. *I wonder how Ashley is doing down there. I hope she's okay.*

Mary-Kate snuggled further into the bed. *I'm not just worried about Ashley,* she realized. *I miss her, too! Amazing!*

CHAPTER ELEVEN

"Let's see," Kevin said as he checked out the twins' lunch bags. "Pickle relish in Ashley's tuna fish, onions in Mary-Kate's."

"You're getting good, Dad," Mary-Kate said. She zipped up her gray hooded sweatshirt and sat down at the breakfast table. Ashley was still upstairs getting ready for school.

"Thanks," Kevin said. He looked up from the counter. "Did you hear that storm last night?"

"Storm?" Mary-Kate said. She grabbed an English muffin and shrugged. "I probably slept through it."

"Mary-Kate Burke?" Kevin said. He raised an eyebrow. "Slept through a thunderstorm?"

"Like Rip van Winkle," Mary-Kate lied. She couldn't let her dad know the truth—that she'd been scared out of her skin.

Kevin smiled. "Nice try, Mary-Kate."

"What do you mean?" Mary-Kate asked.

"I know how you get in a thunderstorm," Kevin said. "And you were alone up in the attic last night."

Mary-Kate shrugged. "You know what they say." She spread jam on her muffin. "The best way to overcome your fear is to face it head on. I must have been cured!"

Kevin tilted his head. "Is that why you're wearing two different-colored socks?"

"Huh?" Mary-Kate said. She looked under the table at her mismatched feet and sighed. She could never fool her dad, so why try now?

"Okay, okay," Mary-Kate sighed. "I guess I had a little trouble sleeping last night. And I did get a few goosebumps here and there."

"Sort of wished Ashley was up there with you?" Kevin asked with a wink.

Mary-Kate smiled. "You win, Dad. Having my own room is kind of lonely. And a little scary, too."

There, Mary-Kate thought. *The truth is out.*

"Then why don't you tell Ashley that you're

starting to miss her?" Kevin urged.

"Dad!" Mary-Kate frowned. "I'd rather chew glass than give in to Ashley. She ditched me for Nicole, remember?"

"I guess that means you're not going to Ashley's ballet recital tomorrow night?" Kevin asked.

"You guessed right," Mary-Kate said.

Kevin shook his head. "You have no idea how sick I am of you girls fighting like this."

I'm sick of it, too, Mary-Kate admitted to herself. *But I refuse to be the first one to give in.*

"Dad?" Mary-Kate said. "Please don't tell Ashley that I missed her last night, okay?"

"I won't," Kevin said. "But I think *you* should tell her!"

Ashley walked into the kitchen wearing a striped turtleneck sweater and a short black skirt. She stopped and sniffed the air. "Are we having spaghetti for breakfast? I smell garlic."

Mary-Kate sank down in her chair. She couldn't understand why she still smelled. Especially after using a whole bottle of strawberry kiwi shower gel.

"Dad must have knocked down the garlic shaker last night," Mary-Kate said quickly. "When he was sneaking one of his late-night snacks."

"I did not!" Kevin insisted. "And I do not sneak late-night snacks."

"Whatever," Ashley said. She sat down next to Mary-Kate and poured herself a glass of orange juice.

"How did you sleep last night, Ashley?" Kevin asked.

"Like a baby, Dad!" Ashley said. She stretched in her chair. "It's amazing what having your own room does for your soul."

Mary-Kate glared at her sister. She was glad she hadn't told Ashley how much she missed her.

"I'm out of here," Mary-Kate said. She dropped her muffin on her plate and picked up her back-pack.

"Aren't you girls going to walk to school together?" Kevin asked. His face softened. "Just like you've done since you were little kids in kindergarten?"

Ashley shook her head. "Nicole is picking me up in a few minutes."

"And I'm walking to school with Max and Brian," Mary-Kate said, heading for the door.

"Wait, Mary-Kate," Kevin said. He held out her lunch bag. "You forgot your tuna sandwich."

"Thanks, Dad," Mary-Kate said. She peeked into

the paper bag. "A bag of chocolate chip cookies, too? Way to go!"

"I hope you put one in my bag, too, Dad," Ashley said.

"Nope," Kevin said. "You two will have to share that one."

Mary-Kate and Ashley looked at each other.

"Clever, Dad," Mary-Kate said. She tossed the cookie bag to her father and opened the front door. "See you after school."

After Mary-Kate left, Ashley continued to eat her breakfast. She noticed her father staring at her.

"Is something wrong, Dad?" she asked.

"Yes," Kevin said. He tilted his head. "Ashley, you have dark rings under your eyes."

"I'm not wearing mascara, Dad," Ashley said. "Honest!"

"I believe you, I believe you," Kevin said. "But I don't believe that you got a good night's sleep."

Busted, Ashley thought.

"Okay, Dad." She sighed. "I hardly slept a wink last night."

"Why not?" Kevin asked.

Ashley sank back in her chair. "It was too quiet."

"Too quiet?" Kevin asked. "It was a tempest out there last night!"

"You don't understand," Ashley said. "When Mary-Kate sleeps, she snores, she tosses, she sometimes even talks in her sleep. You wouldn't believe what she once said about that hunky substitute teacher—"

"I don't want to hear it," Kevin said, holding up his hand.

"Anyway," Ashley went on. "I was always able to fall asleep to the sounds of Mary-Kate."

Kevin leaned over the table. "Does that mean you're not mad at her anymore?" he asked in a hopeful voice.

Ashley thought about the trick Mary-Kate played on her. And about the party.

"Oh, I'm still mad," Ashley said. "But I guess I do miss having her around."

"Then why don't you tell her?" Kevin asked.

Ashley sat up in her chair. She couldn't tell Mary-Kate. That would be giving in! Surrendering! Waving the white flag!

"Dad, how can I?" Ashley asked. "She tried to break up my friendship with Nicole."

Kevin shook his head.

"Ashley, what good is it if the two of you miss

each other, but won't admit it to each other?"

The two of us? Ashley thought. *Wait a minute!*

"Dad?" Ashley asked. "Does Mary-Kate miss me? Did she say anything to you?"

Kevin blushed a deep shade of red. He began fumbling with his briefcase. "You know, I had no idea how late it was. And I think I left all my work in the living room."

Ashley watched as her dad hurried out of the kitchen.

Maybe it's true, Ashley thought. *Maybe Mary-Kate misses me, too.*

But if she does, why doesn't she show it?

CHAPTER TWELVE

"Remember, girls," Madame Suzette said. She clapped her manicured hands. "The first performance in the recital will be 'The Black Swan Pas de Deux' from *Swan Lake*."

Ashley glanced over at her dance teacher. She was standing backstage in a fancy pink suit with a corsage on the lapel.

"*Swan Lake*," Melissa Potts whispered. She flapped her arms in the air. "That's us!"

Ashley nodded excitedly. She and Melissa were sitting on the floor, stretching their legs. They were dressed in white leotards, sheer white skirts, and feathered headpieces.

Amelia Gomez sat down on the floor next to

them. She was dancing the part of a swan, too.

"How can we dance with feathers on our heads?" Amelia griped. She plucked a white feather from her headpiece and blew it into the air. "It's a good thing I'm not allergic."

"Hey, it could be worse," Melissa said. "We could be wrapped in gauze like that goofy dance company I saw on TV— what's their name?"

Ashley rolled her eyes.

"They're the Todd Tyler Dance Company, and they are not goofy!" Ashley said. Then she chuckled. "For a moment you sounded just like my sister, Mary-Kate."

"Speaking of Mary-Kate, where is she?" Melissa asked. "She's always backstage before your recitals to wish you luck."

"Um, Mary-Kate hasn't been feeling too well lately," Ashley said, trying to make an excuse.

"Really?" Amelia asked. "What's wrong with her?"

"Um, she has, er . . ." Ashley had to think of something fast. "Uh—twinfluenza."

"Twinfluenza?" Amelia gasped. "Sounds serious."

"Is it contagious?" Melissa asked.

"Very!" Ashley said.

She was hoping Mary-Kate would come to the recital. But it didn't look good. Her sister had spent the whole day studying math in her attic room. When Ashley and Kevin left the house, Mary-Kate and Carrie were in the middle of a serious game of poker.

"Attention, my little swans!" Madame Suzette called in her thick French accent. "A dozen roses have just arrived for a lucky dancer."

Excited whispers filled the backstage area. Who were they for?

Madame Suzette looked at the small card that was tucked in with the bouquet. "And they are for . . ."

Ashley stared at the roses in her dance teacher's arms. They were yellow—just like the kind Mary-Kate always brought her.

She's here, Ashley thought, standing up. *Mary-Kate came to my recital!*

"Vanessa Pennypacker!" Madame Suzette announced. "Our prima ballerina in the show!"

Ashley froze.

"For me?" Vanessa shrieked. She jumped up and down so hard some of her black feathers fluttered off. "No way! No way!"

Ashley watched Vanessa take the yellow roses from Madame Suzette.

"Who are they from?" Madame Suzette asked.

Vanessa clutched the card to her chest. "They're from my most adoring fans!" she said dramatically.

Melissa rolled her eyes. "That means they're from her mom and dad," she whispered.

Ashley was happy for Vanessa—but sad for herself.

While Melissa and Amelia continued their leg stretches, Ashley walked over to the curtain. Pulling the edge aside, she peeked out into the audience.

The theater was filled with guests. Ashley saw her dad in the second row. There was someone sitting next to him. Was it Mary-Kate?

Ashley stretched her neck to see. It wasn't her sister at all. It was Nicole, and she didn't even bring flowers!

Why did I ever suggest this dumb twin divorce? Ashley thought sadly. *And how can I dance like a graceful swan—when I feel like a total turkey?*

CHAPTER THIRTEEN

"Good morning, Madame Swan!" Nicole said the next morning. "Did your feet touch the ground yet?"

Ashley stood at the back door and yawned. She didn't expect Nicole to come by so early on a Sunday.

"Hi, Nicole," Ashley said through her yawn.

"You were soooo great," Nicole babbled on. "I was thinking of taking ballet lessons myself. Maybe I'll even be in your class. This way we can go together after school. Wouldn't that be cool?"

"Way cool," Ashley said. But after she rubbed the sleep out of her eyes, she gasped.

Nicole was wearing the exact same striped

sweater and drawstring pants that Ashley had on!

"Nicole," Ashley said. She pointed to her own clothes. "You were with me at the mall when I bought this outfit."

"I know," Nicole said, twirling around. "I liked it so much I went back and bought it for myself."

"Nicole, wearing the same clothes as your friends was cute in kindergarten," Ashley complained. "But in seventh grade—it's tacky."

"You're forgetting something, Ashley," Nicole said. "We're not just *friends* anymore. We're twins!"

"Nicole," Ashley said slowly. "Wearing the same clothes isn't what being a twin is all about."

"I know," Nicole said. "That's why I'm going to start combing my hair like you. I'm even going to put pickle relish in my tuna fish from now on."

Ashley felt herself starting to panic. Nicole was a good friend, but she was taking this twin thing too far. Way too far!

"Watch this, Ashley," Nicole said. She squeezed her eyes shut. Then she pressed her fingers against her head.

"What are you doing?" Ashley asked.

"Shh. I'm trying to read your mind," Nicole said. "That's a twin thing, too, right?"

Ashley stared at Nicole as she swayed back and forth.

"Mmm. Mmm. Mmm," Nicole hummed. "I am entering the Psychic Twin Zone!"

It was more than Ashley could take.

"Cut it out, Nicole!" she demanded. "Cut it out, right now!"

Nicole's eyes popped open. "Why?"

Ashley waved her arms in the air. "Because twins are twins. They are not clones!"

Silence.

Nicole looked startled. Ashley *felt* startled. She had just admitted that it was a good thing for twins to be different!

"Does that mean you don't want to dress alike anymore?" Nicole asked. "Or wear our hair the same way?"

Ashley took a deep breath. Then she nodded.

"Mary-Kate and I don't even dress alike or wear our hair the same," Ashley said. "And we're *really* twins."

Nicole looked hurt and confused.

"But we had so much fun together, Ashley," Nicole said. "We have so much in common."

"We can still have fun," Ashley said. "But as friends, not sisters."

Nicole stared down at her shoes. "I always wanted a sister. Especially a twin sister."

"I know, Nicole," Ashley said. "But having great friends is important, too. I mean, you can't have a whole sleepover with only your twin, right?"

"Yeah," Nicole said slowly.

"And we can't borrow each other's clothes if we keep dressing alike, right?" Ashley asked.

"I guess," Nicole sighed. Then she smiled. "Do you still want to be my friend, Ashley?"

"Sure!" Ashley said. "Who else likes ballet as much as I do? And cheesecake? And—"

"And Kyle Martin!" Nicole blurted.

Ashley frowned. "You like Kyle Martin, too? Since when?"

"Only kidding!" Nicole laughed. She turned away from the door. "I'll be right back." ·

"Where are you going?" Ashley asked.

"To change my clothes," Nicole smiled. "This sweater itches. And to be honest—pickle relish makes me gag."

As Ashley watched Nicole walk away, Carrie walked into the kitchen.

"Good morning, Ashley," Carrie looked at the cereal bowl on the table. "You didn't eat your Squirrel Nuts."

"I'm stashing it away for the winter," Ashley joked. "That natural stuff doesn't fly with me."

Carrie smiled. "In that case, I'll make you a nice un-organic Pop-Tart."

Ashley glanced around the kitchen for Mary-Kate. Where was she this morning?

"Ashley, I heard from your dad how well you danced last night," Carrie said. "I'm sorry I couldn't be there."

"That's okay, Carrie," Ashley said. "I know you had to stay home with Mary-Kate. What did you two do last night anyway?"

"Let's see," Carrie said. "We played poker. And Scrabble. Then I burned a meditation candle . . . and melted pizza muffins in the microwave."

Carrie tapped her chin. "Or did I burn the pizza muffins or melt the—oh, well, we had fun."

"Um, Carrie?" Ashley said slowly. "Where is Mary-Kate? Not that I really care . . . I was just wondering if I could have her Pop-Tart."

"She's shooting hoops with your dad," Carrie said. She dropped a Pop-Tart in the toaster. "Her big basketball game is this afternoon. Are you going?"

Ashley shook her head. "No way. She didn't come to my ballet recital last night. So why should I root for her?"

80

Carrie sat down at the table across from Ashley.

"You know, I think Mary-Kate was thinking about you last night," Carrie said with a gentle smile.

Ashley looked up. "She was? How do you know?"

"While we were playing Scrabble, she kept looking at the clock," Carrie said. "I think she was waiting for you to come home."

Ashley sighed. "Or she was waiting for *South Park* to start."

"Maybe," Carrie said. "But if you ask me, I think she really misses you. And if I'm not mistaken . . . I think you kind of miss her, too."

"Not really," Ashley said quickly. But then her shoulders dropped. She was tired of playing the "I don't care" game.

Ashley sighed. "Yeah. I do kind of miss her. And just a few minutes ago I realized something pretty important."

"What?" Carrie asked. She caught the Pop-Tart as it flew out of the toaster.

"That it's *okay*!" Ashley declared. "It's okay that Mary-Kate and I are so different. In fact, that's what makes it so much fun! You know, Nicole wanted to be my twin, too. But only one person can really be that. Mary-Kate!"

Carrie walked over to Ashley. She placed the Pop-Tart on a plate in front of her. Then she gave her a hug.

"I think you figured out something very important. Thanks for being so honest with me," Carrie said. "Now, how about being honest with Mary-Kate?"

"You mean wave the white flag?" Ashley cried. "Carrie, after all that's happened, I wouldn't even know how."

Ashley munched silently for a few moments. Getting her feelings off her chest made her feel better. But she still had a long way to go.

"Hey, I know," Carrie said. "Why don't you surprise Mary-Kate by showing up at her basketball game today?"

"Basketball?" Ashley cried. "Sit in a smelly gym while a bunch of jocks fight over some ball? No way!"

"Mary-Kate is one of those jocks," Carrie reminded her. "That's what makes her different from you, remember?"

Ashley frowned. "I remember."

"Besides," Carrie said. "I went to my share of basketball games myself in high school. You can even say I was part of the team."

"*You?*" Ashley asked. "Played basketball?"

"Nope," Carrie said. She put one hand on her hip and the other in the air. "But I was a pretty mean cheerleader!"

Ashley giggled. She tried to picture Carrie wearing a letter sweater and doing a split.

"Okay, I'll go," Ashley finally said. "But I'm warning you, Carrie. I don't know the first thing about basketball."

Carrie waved her hand. "It's a piece of cake. I'll even lend you *Basketball for Dummies*. Then you'll know the difference between a tackle and a touchdown."

"Carrie!" Ashley laughed. "I'm not that dumb. I know that a touchdown is for hockey, right?"

Carrie looked nervous. "You've *got* to be kidding!"

"I am!" Ashley smiled.

She wanted to go to Mary-Kate's game, but deep down inside she was worried. What if it didn't work? What if Mary-Kate saw her and told her to get lost?

"If I'm going to the game tonight," Ashley thought out loud, "then I'd better bring some kind of peace offering."

"Like what?" Carrie asked.

"I don't know," Ashley shrugged. "Roses?"

"Roses at a basketball game?" Carrie exclaimed. She shook her head. "Definitely *not* cool!"

"I've got to do something to break the ice!" Ashley said. She propped her elbows on the table and rested her chin in her hands. "But what?"

"Beats me," Carrie said. She walked over to Kevin's coffee machine and poured herself a cup. She said a little cheer under her breath. "Ricka racka firecracker sis boom bah. Central High . . . Central High . . . rah, rah, rah."

Ashley sat up in her seat.

Rah? Rah? Rah?

"That's it!" Ashley said. "If I can't say it with flowers, I'll cheer it instead!"

Carrie looked up from her cup of coffee. "I'm not quite sure I know where you're going with this."

"I'll explain everything, Carrie," Ashley said. "But first . . . do you still have your pom-poms?"

CHAPTER FOURTEEN

"I don't know, Mary-Kate," Pamela Lopez said in a low voice. "I have this weird feeling that we're going to lose."

Mary-Kate glanced up from fastening her basketball sneakers.

"Come on, Pamela. Where's your team spirit?" Mary-Kate said. "We're the Red Hot Salamanders. Who can beat us?"

Pamela pointed to a group of tall girls in green T-shirts entering the gym. "The Jolly Green Giants!" she moaned.

"Whoops." Mary-Kate gulped as she watched the tall team slam down their backpacks. "Know what? I have a weird feeling that you're right."

Pamela picked up a basketball and twirled it on her finger. "Want to practice?" she asked. "We're going to need it."

"In a sec," Mary-Kate said. "There's something I have to do first."

While Pamela dribbled the ball around the court, Mary-Kate turned toward the bleachers. Looking up, she saw her dad waving from the middle row. But no matter how hard she looked, she couldn't see Ashley anywhere.

My game won't be the same without Ashley, Mary-Kate thought. *I'm going to miss her sitting in the bleachers and holding her nose.*

But Mary-Kate couldn't blame her sister for not coming to the game. After all, she didn't go to Ashley's ballet recital last night.

"All players on the court!" Coach Kiyoko called out. "Red Hots—let's go!"

Mary-Kate joined her team in front of Coach Kiyoko.

"Okay, here are the positions for the first game," the coach said, looking down at a clipboard. "Pamela and Louise will be the guards. Julia and Anne will be forwards. And Mary-Kate, you'll take center. Everybody got it?"

"Got it," the Red Hots said together.

"The game doesn't start for a few minutes. So let's warm up with some passes," Coach Kiyoko said. She passed the ball to Julia. Julia passed the ball to Anne. But just as Anne passed the ball to Mary-Kate . . .

"RICKA RACKA FIRECRACKER, SIS, BOOM, BAH!"

"Huh?" Mary-Kate said. The ball flew over her shoulder as she whirled around. She stared at the end of the court and gasped.

Standing in a short red skirt and a white sweater was Ashley! She had bells on her sneakers and was waving two red pom-poms in the air.

"MARY-KATE! MARY-KATE! RAH! RAH! RAH!"

Ashley leaped in the air with the pom-poms. After she landed in a split, she gave Mary-Kate a huge grin.

"Ashley!" Mary-Kate whispered under her breath. She felt a glow of happiness.

"Mary-Kate?" Coach Kiyoko shouted. "Are you still with us?"

"Yes!" Mary-Kate said, snapping around. "But could you excuse me for a second, Coach? Um . . . my sneaker. It keeps . . . untying."

"You're wearing Velcro!" Coach Kiyoko said.

Then she nodded. "Okay, okay, but just for a second."

"Thanks, Coach!" Mary-Kate said. She ran over to her sister, grinning.

"Hey, with a jump like that, you should be shooting hoops!" she said.

Ashley swung her pom-pom. "Those ballet lessons aren't for nothing, you know."

"Ballet," Mary-Kate sighed. "I really wish I went to your ballet recital last night."

"I wish you'd been there, too," Ashley admitted. "It wasn't the same without you yawning in the audience."

Mary-Kate and Ashley giggled. Then they looked at each other and took a deep breath.

"*I'm sorry!*" they said at the same time.

Laughing, Mary-Kate grabbed Ashley's hands.

"I shouldn't have dumped you like that," Ashley said.

"And I shouldn't have been mad at you for being friends with Nicole," Mary-Kate said. "You have every right to have your own friends."

Ashley put her arm around Mary-Kate's shoulder. "Yeah, but you'll always be my *best* bud!"

Mary-Kate was so happy she felt as if she could burst.

But she was also a little embarrassed.

"Hey!" Mary-Kate warned. She pulled herself out from under Ashley's arm. "Don't get sappy on me here. The Green Giants will eat me alive!"

"Yo, Mary-Kate!" Coach Kiyoko called. She blasted her whistle. "The game's going to start!"

"Coming, Coach!" Mary-Kate called. She turned to Ashley. "After the game let's celebrate, okay?"

"But what if you lose?" Ashley asked.

"We're not celebrating the game, Ashley," Mary-Kate said. "We're celebrating our truce! Our treaty! Our peace agreement!"

"Cool!" Ashley said. "And I know a fabulous place for cheesecake!"

"Cheesecake?" Mary-Kate smiled. "You know, I always wanted to try cheesecake."

As Mary-Kate ran back to the court she gave her dad a thumbs-up sign. He grinned back.

It felt good to be in the game.

And it felt *great* to be a twin!

Mary-Kate & Ashley's Scrapbook

My sister Ashley and I usually get along great—except for one time when Ashley got a new friend named Nicole. Soon she was doing everything with Nicole, and not with me. I felt really left out.

So I called Nicole and asked her to come over.

Then I dressed up like Ashley and told Nicole I didn't want to be her friend anymore.

Ashley was pretty
mad. In fact, she
was really furious!

We decided to split up.
I moved out of my
bedroom—into my
very own attic pent-
house.

I even had a party and didn't invite Ashley.

But it was scary in the attic!
I decided I didn't want to
sleep there after all!

Besides, I sort of missed
Ashley. And it turned
out she sort of missed
me, too.

So now we're back
together again. And it's
never been better!

PSST! Take a sneak peek
at

Let's Party!

Ashley burst into the house and headed straight for her dad. He was sitting on the couch, watching a basketball game with Mary-Kate and Carrie.

"Hi, Dad," she said. "I need to ask you something really important." She turned the sound down on the TV. "Can I have a surprise party for Jennifer's birthday?"

"When?" Kevin Burke asked. His eyes darted from her face to the TV and back.

"Saturday night, two weeks from today," Ashley answered.

Kevin thought for a moment, then shook his head. "I'm sorry, Ashley," he answered. "We can't have two parties here on the same night."

"Two parties!" Ashley yelped. "Why two parties? Who's giving the other one?"

Mary-Kate turned and looked at her. "That would be me," she said.

"You're giving a party?" Ashley's mouth dropped open. "Since when?"

"I just decided today," Mary-Kate explained. "Dad said it was okay. It's a surprise party for Amanda. Her birthday is that week."

"But you can't!" Ashley exclaimed. "I mean, I have this all planned!"

"Calm down, Ashley." Kevin Burke turned off the TV. "Why can't you choose another night?"

"Because Jennifer's birthday is that week, too," Ashley replied. "And on Friday night we have tickets to go to the *Nutcracker*, remember?"

Kevin looked thoughtful. "Maybe you can have one big party—together," he suggested.

Ashley looked at Mary-Kate. "Maybe. Here's what I was thinking. We get everyone to dress up, we put on some great music for dancing, we serve Sprite in fancy glasses. It will be so—"

"So *not* Amanda," Mary-Kate interrupted. "Besides, if we get all dressed up, how are we supposed to play Twister, Ping-Pong, and air hockey?"

Ashley screwed up her face. "Twister?" she said. "Whose idea is that?"

"Mine," Mary-Kate answered. "And video games. And Pin the Tail on the Chicago Bulls—just for kicks. It's so goofy, Amanda will love it."

Ashley shook her head. "Jennifer would faint if anyone played those—those *babyish* games at her birthday party," she said. "Her party has to be sophisticated and elegant. I've got it all planned."

"You've got it planned for next year," Mary-Kate said. "Because we're not doing any of that stuff *this* year. Not at Amanda's party."

Carrie spoke up for the first time. "I have an idea. Ashley, what if you have your fancy dance upstairs, in the living room. And Mary-Kate—you could have your bash downstairs in my apartment!"

"Really?" Ashley asked. Her eyes lit up.

Not a bad idea, Mary-Kate thought. The basement was the best place to play Twister and air hockey. Mary-Kate knew her dad would have a fit if they started tossing stuff around in the living room.

"Okay, it's a deal," Mary-Kate told Ashley.

"Thank you!" Ashley screamed. She leaned over and gave her sister a hug. "Now I can get a new dress!"

Mary-Kate laughed. "All I have to do is make sure my favorite jeans are clean. But I'll make you a bet," she added.

"What's that?" Ashley asked.

"I'll bet my party is a lot more fun than yours," Mary-Kate declared.

"Oh, right." Ashley rolled her eyes. "Twister and Pin the Tail? Can't wait."

"Just you wait and see," Mary-Kate said. "My friends are going to have an awesome time."

Ashley shrugged. "Whatever. You do your thing, Mary-Kate. And I'll do mine. And may the best party win!"

PARTY IN STYLE

WITH MARY-KATE AND ASHLEY!

You'll go *simply wild* for their all-new video!

You're Invited to MARY-KATE & ASHLEY'S™
FASHION PARTY™

Each video includes a
Mary-Kate and Ashley
sampler book from
Parachute/Harper.

DUALSTAR VIDEO

KidVision
A DIVISION OF
WarnerVision
ENTERTAINMENT

**Load up
the one horse
open sleigh.
Mary-Kate and Ashley's
Christmas Album
is on the way.**

It doesn't matter if you live around the corner...
or around the world....
If you are a fan of Mary-Kate and Ashley Olsen,
you should be a member of

Mary-Kate + Ashley's Fun Club™

Here's what you get
Our Funzine™
An autographed color photo
Two black and white individual photos
A full sized color poster
An official Fun Club™ membership card
A Fun Club™ School folder
Two special Fun Club™ surprises
Fun Club™ Collectible Catalog
Plus a Fun Club™ box to keep everything in.

To join Mary-Kate + Ashley's Fun Club™, fill out the form below
and send it along with

U.S. Residents	$17.00
Canadian Residents	$22.00 (US Funds only)
International Residents	$27.00 (US Funds only)

Mary-Kate + Ashley's Fun Club™
859 Hollywood Way, Suite 275
Burbank, CA 91505

Name:_____

Address:_____

City:_____ St:_____ Zip:_____

Phone: (_____) _____

E-Mail:_____

Check us out on the web at
www.marykateandashley.com